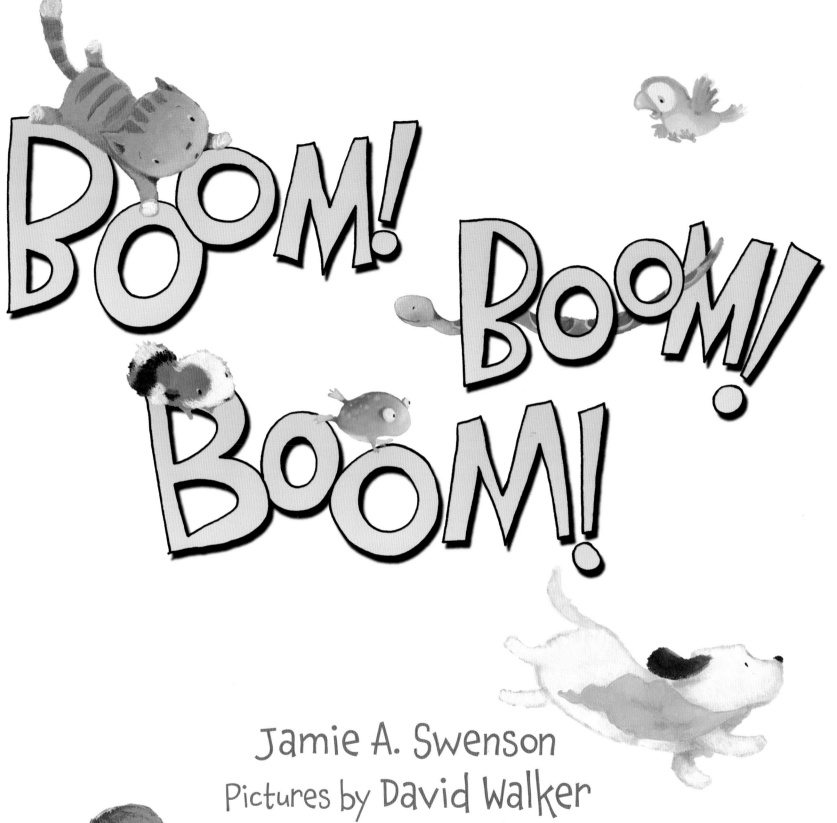

BOOM! BOOM! BOOM! BOOM!

Jamie A. Swenson
Pictures by David Walker

FARRAR STRAUS GIROUX
New York

One stormy night, I jumped into bed.
Safe with a book and my bear named Fred.

FLASH! CRASH!

BOOM! BOOM! BOOM!

"Arrooo," howled dog. "Is there room?"
"Jump in," I said. "There's room for two.
Fred for me and blankie for you."

Two snuggled together to wait out the storm.
Dog and I all comfy and warm.

FLASH! CRASH!
BOOM! BOOM!
BOOM!

"Yowl," mewed kitty. "Is there room?"
"Cuddle in," I said. "There's room for three.
A dog, a cat, and little ol' me."

Three burrowed under all comfy-cozy.
That's when I felt a twitchy nosey.

"*Eeee Eeee,*" squealed guinea pig. "Is there room?"
"Of course," I said. "There's room for four."
Outside, the storm continued to roar.

We four nestled and listened to the rain.
Split, splat, splat, splop, a stormy refrain.

"*Ribbet,*" croaked frog. "Is there room?"
"Boing in," I said. "But then, no hopping.
With five, this bed is tip-flip-flopping!"

Five smushed friends jostled and jammed,
As the storm bellowed and bammed.

FLASH! CRASH! BOOM! BOOM! BOOM! BOOM!

"Squawk," shrieked parrot. "Is there room?"
"Oh dear," I said. "I guess we'll try.
But if we crash, be ready to fly!"

Six of us were packed in tight.
I prayed my bed would last the night.

"*Hhhhhhhisssssssssss,*" hissed snake. "Isssss there room?"
"Slide in," I said. "At least you're thin."
The storm raged with a thunderous din.

Snake coiled up—a bit too snug.
Seven squished folks in a reptile hug.

FLASH! BOOM! BOOM!
CRASH!! BOOM!

"No fair!" cried Sis. "Is there room?"
"Enough!" I said. "You have your *own* bed!
If you push in, there's no room for Fred!"

Sis jumped in with elbows flying—
The bed groaned, AND creaked, AND THEN stopped trying!

Squawk!

Bed now broken, they scattered—they flew.
Alone again, I knew just what to do.

Arrooo!

Ribbet!

Fluffing my pillow, I jumped into bed.
Just me, a book, and my bear named Fred.

Fluffing my pillow, I jumped into bed.
Just me, a book, and my bear named Fred.

For Mom, Jon, Addie, and Norah,
who see me through all life's storms —J.S.

Especially for my very brave friend Lucas —D.W.

Farrar Straus Giroux Books for Young Readers
175 Fifth Avenue, New York 10010

Text copyright © 2013 by Jamie A. Swenson
Pictures copyright © 2013 by David Walker
All rights reserved
Color separations by Bright Arts (H.K.) Ltd.
Printed in China by Toppan Leefung Printers Ltd.,
Dongguan City, Guangdong Province
Designed by Roberta Pressel
First edition, 2013
1 3 5 7 9 10 8 6 4 2

mackids.com

Library of Congress Cataloging-in-Publication Data
Swenson, Jamie.
    Boom! boom! boom! / Jamie A. Swenson ; pictures by David Walker. — 1st ed.
        p.   cm.
    Summary: On a stormy night, a child snuggles into bed with a book and a teddy bear
but is soon joined by one dog, one cat, and more until the child, and the bed, reach their
limit.
    ISBN 978-0-374-30868-1
    [1. Stories in rhyme.   2. Storms—Fiction.   3. Bedtime—Fiction.   4. Counting.]
I. Walker, David, 1965–   ill.   II. Title.

PZ8.3.S99558Boo 2013
[E]—dc23
                                                                                2011035444